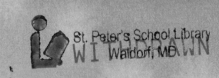

The Little Mermaid

Illustrated by
Francesca Salucci

Based upon the story
by Hans Christian Andersen

McGraw-Hill
Children's Publishing

McGraw-Hill
Children's Publishing

A Division of The **McGraw·Hill** Companies

This edition published in the United States in 2002 by
McGraw-Hill Children's Publishing,
A Division of The McGraw-Hill Companies
8787 Orion Place
Columbus, Ohio 43240

www.MHkids.com

ISBN 1-58845-477-0

Library of Congress Cataloging-in-Publication Data is on file with the publisher.

10 9 8 7 6 5 4 3 2 1 CHRT 06 05 04 03 02

Printed in China.

The Little Mermaid

Illustrated by
Francesca Salucci

Deep in the ocean, the sea king and his three lovely daughters lived in a great underwater castle. These princesses of the sea were mermaids with shimmering tails and beautiful voices.

The princesses were happy, playing and exploring with the sea creatures they had known since childhood. But most of all, they loved to hear their grandmother's stories of the surface world far above them. Each day the princesses gathered around their grandmother and her magic crystal, which showed them the human world, a strange and magical place where people breathed air instead of water.

Marina, the youngest princess, longed to visit the surface world.

Her grandmother saw this and understood. "I was just as adventuresome as you were once," she told Marina. "I, too, wanted to visit far away places and to see wondrous things, but you are still too young to leave our underwater kingdom. The surface world can be very dangerous. For now, the best place for you is here with your family."

Marina loved her grandmother and knew that she was very wise, but Marina continued to dream.

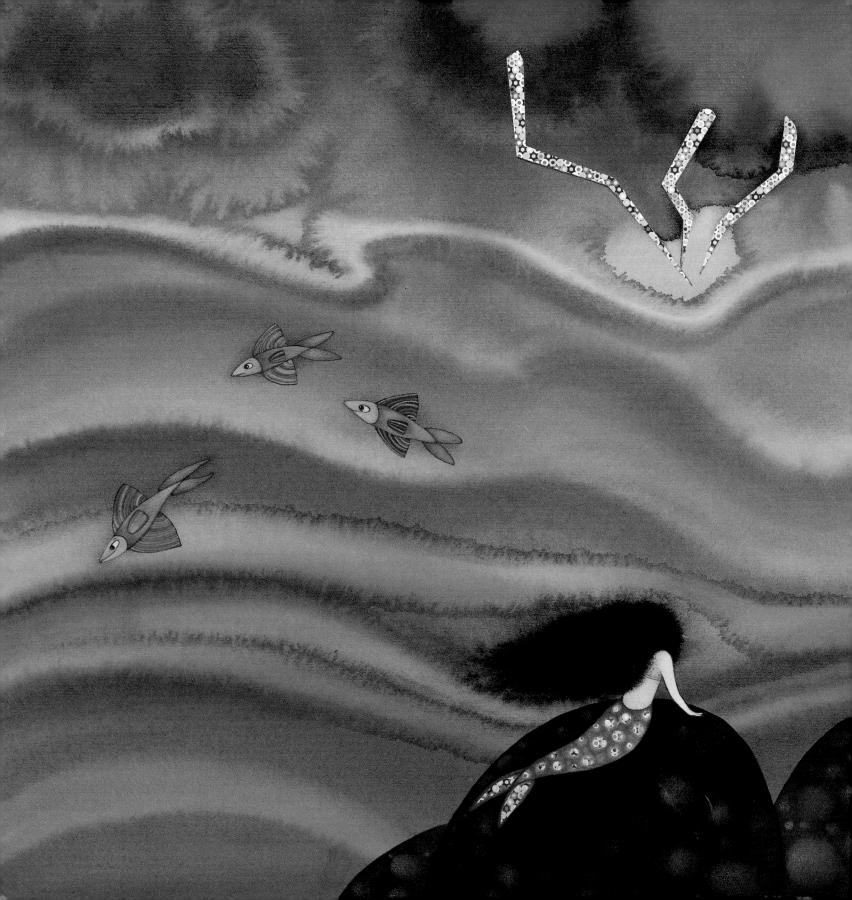

One day, her curiosity overcame her, and Marina disobeyed her grandmother. She swam up and up, until she finally broke through the waves. With a gasp, she took in her first breath of air. It smelled salty and fresh, and Marina laughed at the way it tickled her nose. The wind was cool as it blew against her face, making her skin tingle. She watched as the white foam of the waves crashed over ragged black rocks that jutted from the water's surface.

Marina looked up. The sky was vast and wide like the sea, but it wasn't blue. It was dark with a fierce storm. And under the sky, a large ship with billowing white sails bobbed on the violent waves.

Marina had never seen such an amazing sight as a ship on the ocean. And though the wind was growing stronger and the sky darker, she wanted to get a better look. She fought her way through the waves and moved closer, peeking though a small porthole in the ship's bow. There stood a handsome young prince that Marina had seen many times in her grandmother's magic crystal.

Suddenly a huge wave washed over the ship and sent it crashing onto the jagged rocks near shore. Wood splintered and cold water rushed into the hull. A moment later, the great vessel disappeared from sight.

Marina knew that the prince could not breathe underwater the way she could, so she dove below the surface and desperately searched for him. Finally, she found him sinking to the bottom and pulled him to the surface as fast as she could.

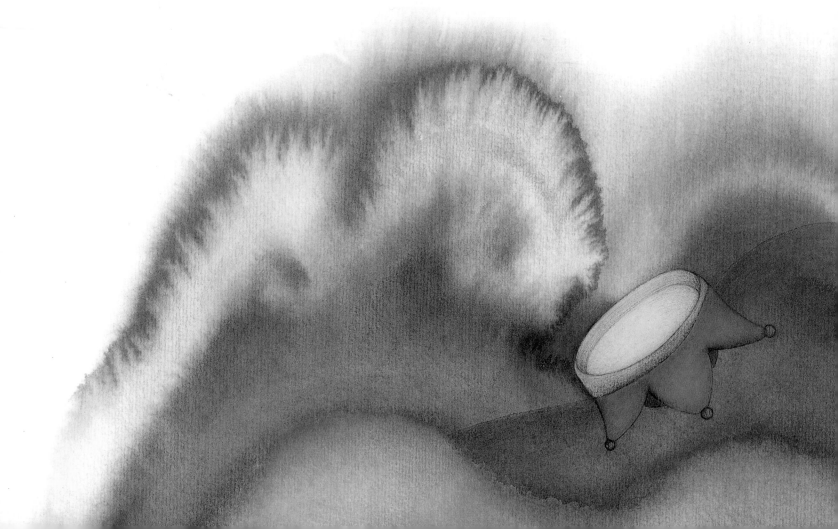

When they broke through the waves, Marina carried the prince to shore. She laid him on the sand and gently brushed the wet hair from his brow. Then she looked down at his handsome face and felt her heart stir.

Suddenly, she saw one of the prince's guards approaching from the nearby castle. She knew that the prince was now safe and that he would be brought home and cared for. Silently, she dove into the ocean and returned home.

Because she had disobeyed her grandmother, Marina was afraid to tell her family about her adventure in the surface world. She could only gaze into her grandmother's crystal ball and secretly watch the handsome prince who had touched her heart. She wondered what it would be like to know him and dreamed of a day when they could be together.

One day, Marina went to visit a sea witch who performed powerful magic. She told the witch about her dream.

"Well, pretty thing," said the witch in a horrible voice. "You want human legs so you can walk with your handsome prince in the surface world, do you? But what do I get in return, hmmm?"

"I will give you anything!" cried Marina.

"What a lovely voice you have," rasped the witch. "I will give you what you desire, but you must give me your voice in return. Drink this potion. Legs will grow and your voice will go! But remember this: You must get that handsome prince of yours to marry you, or you will be turned into sea spray!"

Marina knew it was her only chance to be with the prince, so she closed her eyes and quickly drank the potion.

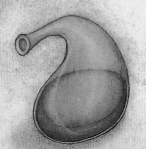

Marina swam to the surface of the water near the prince's castle. As she drew close to shore, her beautiful, shimmering tail disappeared and human legs grew in its place. She stepped out of the water and took a few uncertain steps. Then she sat on a nearby rock and breathed in the fresh air. She felt the warm sun shining on her face. What a marvelous world!

Just then, Marina saw the prince strolling along the beach toward her.

"My dear lady!" said the prince surprised. "How is it that you have come to this shore?"

Marina smiled and touched her lovely throat.

"Oh, you cannot speak," said the prince. "Are you lost? Has the mighty ocean washed you onto this beach?"

Marina nodded.

"Well you are lost no longer," said the prince. "You will be a guest at my castle, and there you may stay as long as it pleases you."

The prince gave Marina beautiful clothes to wear and a soft bed to sleep in. And although Marina could not speak, she and the prince were very happy. They walked together on the beach. They danced and played games. And each evening, the prince read his favorite books to Marina. As time passed, they grew more and more fond of each other.

Marina tried to make the prince understand who she was and where she was from. She painted pictures of her home beneath the waves, of her father the sea king, and of a ship being tossed by a terrible storm. The prince thought her paintings were charming, but he did not understand.

Then one sad day, the prince received a letter from his father, the king. During his travels the king had arranged for his son to marry a princess from a faraway land.

Marina felt that her heart was breaking, but she accompanied the prince on horseback to his bride's homeland to share in his wedding day.

After the ceremony, the wedding party boarded a ship for a celebration. The ship was filled with musicians, dancers, entertainers, and delicious foods. But as the other guests enjoyed themselves, Marina sat alone and cried, knowing that at dawn she would turn into sea spray, as the sea witch had warned.

Suddenly, her sisters called from the water below.

"My sweet Marina!" said one sister. "Do not give up hope! We have been to the sea witch. If you can convince the prince to love you before the first light of dawn, you may keep your legs and remain here forever. If you don't, your fate is sealed."

Marina's heart filled with hope. She stole into the prince's room and crept to the side of his bed. The prince and his lovely new bride were sleeping peacefully side by side. They looked so happy that Marina decided that she could not cause the prince pain by making him choose between her and his wife. Nor would she have him risk the disappointment of his father, or the anger of the people in his kingdom.

Marina leaned over the sleeping prince and kissed him. Then she sadly walked away.

Marina ran to the ship's deck and leapt into the ocean. She looked at her body and saw with joy that her human legs were gone and her own beautiful, shining tail had returned. All around her, mermaids and mermen laughed and talked happily.

"You have made the right choice, Marina," said a young merman at her side. "You have made the ultimate sacrifice for love." He smiled.

Marina and her new friends rose to the water's surface, then higher and higher into the sky. Her body had grown transparent.

"Where are we going?" Marina asked the kind merman beside her.

"We are going home," he said.

And Marina did not feel sad; she felt happy and full of love. She was now a beautiful burst of sea spray, heading skyward toward the home of all good souls.

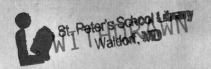